W9-ATZ-652

Stinkers

A novelization by Francine Hughes
From the screenplay by
Bob Wolterstorff and Mike Scott

SCHOLASTIC INC.
New York   Toronto   London   Auckland   Sydney

10 9 8 7 6 5 4 3 2 1   7 8 9/9 0 1 2/0

Printed in the U.S.A.   40

First Scholastic printing, July 1997

1

It was an ordinary day at Dartmoor Academy. The sun was shining. A gentle breeze was blowing.

A banner swayed back and forth. The words "Summer Enrichment Program" rippled in the wind.

Vroom! Roy, the groundskeeper, grinned. He revved his supercharged lawn mower. Vroom! Vroom! He made a sharp right turn. A sharp left turn. He spun the wheel wide. Then he double-backed. Satisfied, he nodded.

Roy had cut a smiling face in the campus lawn.

Inside the auditorium, students were trying to sing. It was opera appreciation. And they were practicing for the Parents' Day show.

Harriet, the music teacher, played the piano. She smiled at the girls and boys. In front of the piano Mr. Brinway, the headmaster, frowned. He held up his arms, leading the song.

"Stop! Stop!" he cried. "Let's try and keep in tune." Annoyed, he banged his baton. The students tried again.

Eight-year-old Sonny DaSilva raised his hand. He crossed his legs and squirmed.

Harriet nodded to excuse him.

Sonny backed out of the auditorium. Immediately, two other hands shot up. Then two more. The students doubled over. Desperate to go.

Harriet waved each one on.

Sonny waited at the top of the stairs. He smoothed back his dark hair. Then he rolled up the sleeves of his T-shirt. Sonny looked tough. He acted tough. But he would do anything for his friends.

Just then Lucy O'Hara skipped over. Her sweet face broke out in a grin. The fun was about to begin!

Allen Witzowitz — Witz for short — stumbled behind Lucy. He wheezed loudly. Then he blew his nose.

Domino Dupree, a wiry African-American, and Lewis "Loaf" Hoover followed on their heels.

Sonny, Lucy, Witz, Domino, and Loaf. Mr. Brinway wished he'd never set eyes on them. He called them troublemakers. Stinkers. But the five friends didn't mind. They liked being Stinkers.

Sonny checked his watch. "Right on schedule."

Nervous, Witz gazed around. "What about Mr. Brinway?" he asked. "Maybe we should really go to the bathroom. You know. Make it look good."

Sonny laughed as the five friends raced

out of the building. "Brinway's too busy singing."

But Mr. Brinway wasn't *that* busy. "Spencer! Max!" the headmaster hissed.

Spencer and Max were big tattletales. And Mr. Brinway had a job for them.

2

The Stinkers hurried to the edge of campus. They ducked inside Roy's shed.

"If Roy catches us, we're dead," Witz said. He peeked outside. No one was around. Good. But what if Roy showed up? What if they got caught?

If there was a reason to be nervous, Witz would find it.

The friends lugged out a big leaf blower. "Roy will think we're stealing," Witz continued. "He'll kill us twice."

"That's impossible," Lucy said matter-offactly. "You would run out of blood."

Blood? Witz opened his eyes wide. He made a strange honking sound.

Sonny snapped his fingers. "Witz? Are you in or out?"

"I'm — I'm — " Witz stammered. Everyone stared at him. "In," he finally said. "I'm in."

"Good." Sonny nodded. "Because you're the test pilot."

"I'm out!" Witz shouted. "I'm out!"

But the Stinkers ignored his protests. Domino gave Witz a noogie and exclaimed, "All right, Witz! You the man!"

"The man's out," said Witz. "Domino! Stop that! I have a headache!"

Spencer and Max poked their heads around the shed. They saw the Stinkers. And the leaf blower. The Stinkers were up to something. Definitely. They raced back to Mr. Brinway.

Meanwhile, the Stinkers went to work. They plunked a helmet on Witz's head. Then they strapped him into a desk chair.

Domino taped a giant kite to the top of the chair.

Loaf fastened the leaf blower to the bottom. Loaf was a mechanical wizard. This was his invention. And he wanted it to be perfect.

"Why me?" Witz moaned.

"Because we voted," Sonny said. "And you were at the doctor's."

Lucy took a paintbrush. She wrote a big "S" for Stinkers on the helmet. "Finished," she said.

"Remember, there's an eject button," Loaf told Witz. "I rigged a rocket under the seat. And a parachute."

"Boy, this is like *Apollo 13*," Domino whispered to Lucy. Domino loved movies. He knew everything about them.

"*Apollo 13?*" Lucy repeated. "Didn't they almost die?"

Witz squeezed his eyes shut. "Tell my mom I loved her," he whimpered.

Loaf cranked the leaf blower. The engine roared. A cloud of smoke blew out. "Three,"

Sonny counted down. "Two. One!"

The blower rattled. The kite shook. Up, up, up it went, taking the blower . . .

Leaving Witz and the chair on the ground.

The blower sliced through the "Summer Enrichment Program" banner. It bumped down to the ground. Then it careened across campus. Up and down. Down and up.

Sonny, Loaf, Lucy, and Domino took off after it.

"This isn't so bad," Witz said, his eyes still closed.

The Stinkers raced back. The blower had turned around.

"Run, Witz!" they shouted.

Witz opened his eyes. It was aiming right for him!

Witz fumbled with the straps. There! He was free! He bolted from the chair — just as the blower nicked the back of it.

Vroom! The blower was closing in. Witz raced up to the others.

The Stinkers ran for the auditorium steps. The door swung open. Mr. Brinway had gotten the report from Spencer and Max. He was coming out to find them.

He saw the Stinkers. Running. Eyes open in terror. He chuckled.

But what was that behind them? Mr. Brinway suddenly choked on his laughter. Whatever it was, was flying right at him!

The Stinkers sped past him onto the porch.

Mr. Brinway dropped to the ground. R-r-r-i-p! The blower buzzed the seat of his pants.

Mr. Brinway stumbled to his feet. Bright red underwear showed from the back of his pants.

The blower zipped past the auditorium. It flew into the playground. The kite caught on the merry-go-round and whipped around.

Mr. Brinway gasped. It was coming at him again! He bolted across campus.

The blower gained ground. It was catching up!

9

Roy gunned his lawn mower. He pulled up beside Mr. Brinway. Just as the blower grazed Mr. Brinway's jacket, Roy tugged the headmaster up onto the lawn mower.

Mr. Brinway panted, out of breath. "What is that thing?"

"I don't know," Roy answered. "But it's heading for your car!"

Mr. Brinway yelped. His fancy new car!

"Don't worry, Mr. Brinway!" Roy shouted. He popped a wheelie. Grass spewed everywhere, but mostly over Mr. Brinway. Then Roy raced ahead of the blower.

Screech! He hit the brakes, right by the car. Mr. Brinway leaped off the mower. He pushed the buttons on his automatic key and the car's convertible top opened, its windshield wipers started, its horn honked, and its alarm went off. He dove into the car.

Nervously, he peered back at the blower. It was too late. It was going to hit! Mr. Brinway braced for the crash.

Put-put-put. The blower sputtered. It stopped in midair. Then it dropped like a rock, missing the car.

Mr. Brinway sighed with relief. It was over. His car was safe. He swung open the door — right into the lawn mower. Crreeesh! He heard the sound of metal being crushed. He saw sparks fly. There was a big ugly hole in the car door.

"Oops" said Roy. "Forgot to turn off the grass cutter."

3

Mr. Brinway called the Stinkers into his office. They stood in a row, at attention. Mr. Brinway paced in front of them. Back and forth. Back and forth. Harriet sat nearby, watching.

"You snuck out of opera appreciation," Mr. Brinway said angrily. "Stole a leaf blower. Damaged my car. Ruined my new seersucker suit."

Mr. Brinway's jacket was hitched up. His red underwear poked through. Lucy giggled.

"Most important," Mr. Brinway went on, "you put a black mark on the Dartmoor name."

"Mr. Brinway," Harriet whispered. "I think you're being too hard on them. They just wanted to have fun."

"Fun, Harriet?" Mr. Brinway hissed back. "Opera appreciation. Now that's fun. This is not summer camp here."

He turned back to the Stinkers. "Now, where was I? Oh yes. You're all expelled."

Lucy groaned. Loaf gasped. Sonny's eyes widened. Witz wheezed. And Domino didn't move. He was too stunned.

"Mr. Brinway," Harriet whispered again. "Remember the board of trustees? The people who make decisions about the school? About you? I don't think they'd like this."

Mr. Brinway thought for a moment.

"What if the newspapers heard about this?" Harriet went on. "The board would fire you. People would point at you and laugh."

"Okay, okay," said Mr. Brinway. "Per-

13

haps I was a little harsh. Children, I'll give you one more chance. But you're on double probation. Step out of line just once and you're history."

Just then Roy knocked at the door. He pushed the desk chair into the room. "Found this behind some bushes," he told Mr. Brinway. "Must have rolled out of your office."

Mr. Brinway rolled his eyes. You couldn't fool him. The Stinkers had taken it. He sat down with a sigh.

"Good thing I disconnected the ejection seat," Loaf whispered.

Boom! The seat shot up. Mr. Brinway exploded out the window. The Stinkers rushed to look outside. The parachute opened, and Mr. Brinway floated to the ground.

"Oh, well," said Loaf. "Guess I didn't disconnect it after all."

Dismissed, the Stinkers trailed after Roy. They wanted to apologize for borrowing his leaf blower. Roy smiled at them. "That's okay. It's cool. You made something fly."

Loaf did some quick figuring. "Next time we'll use more tape," he said. "And one of the lighter five-year-olds."

Beep, beep. A car horn honked. Parents were coming to pick up their children. The school day was over. Students rushed across campus.

Mr. Brinway groaned as he lifted a megaphone. He felt sore from his fall.

"Attention, Dartmoor children," he announced. "Our aquarium trip is tomorrow. And remember. No consent form? No trip."

Witz stood off to the side, waiting for his mom. Uh-oh, he thought. Trouble heading this way!

Spencer and Max strode over.

"How does it feel to be a loser?" Spencer said nastily.

"I'm not a loser. I'm a test pilot." Witz tried to explain.

"All you Stinkers are losers," Max jeered.

Spencer laughed and grabbed Witz's backpack. "What a cheap, dorky thing." He flipped it upside down and jiggled it. Books, papers, and pens tumbled out. "Oops," said Spencer. "Guess it wasn't closed."

He edged closer to Witz.

Suddenly, Sonny stepped in between them. "Pick it up," he told Spencer.

"Why don't you make him?" Max said.

"Maybe we will," Loaf shot back. He jumped next to Sonny.

"Stinkers rule! Others drool!" Lucy popped out from behind Loaf.

Domino crept along the ground. He crawled close to Max. Grinning, he tied a string around Max's backpack. Then he tied the other end to a nearby car.

Spencer smirked. "Hit me and you'll break probation." He sauntered off. Max turned to follow. At that same instant, the car pulled away.

"Huh?" said Max. The car yanked his backpack off his shoulders.

Domino jumped up and smiled. "Now how did that happen?" he asked.

Max chased his backpack down the street. Spencer shrugged. Then he climbed into his father's car.

"Look!" Mr. Brinway told Harriet excitedly. "It's Spencer Dane, Sr. Spencer's dad. That man is worth a fortune. *He* should be on the board of trustees. Then he would give money for my Brinway Music Festival."

Mr. Brinway rushed up to the expensive black car. Smiling, he tapped on the window.

The car peeled away.

"Don't worry, Mr. Dane!" Mr. Brinway called. "We'll talk later!"

17

4

The next day, Roy drove the Dartmoor bus to the Springfield Aquarium. A black van was pulling into the parking lot, too.

Anthony Boccoli squeezed out of the van's front door. He slicked back his greasy black hair. He pushed up his thick black glasses. Then he knocked at the door of the employees' entrance.

A teenager named Tag cracked open the door. "You got the money?" he whispered.

Boccoli waved the money in his face.

Tag nodded. "Meet me by the loading

dock. The sea lion will be waiting."

Meanwhile, Mr. Brinway led everyone inside the aquarium. He herded the students up to a display on a wall. Peering at an information card, he began to read . . . and read . . . and read.

The Stinkers yawned.

"That's fronds," Mr. Brinway said. "F . . . R . . . O . . . N . . . D . . . S, for those of you taking notes."

The Stinkers moved to the back of the group.

"Field trips are supposed to be fun," Domino whispered.

Sonny gazed around, bored. "Where do they keep the killer whales?" he wondered.

"Killer whales," Lucy echoed. "Yeah. Where are they?"

"I think we should stay here," Witz said quickly. "And move when Mr. Brinway says move. How many are with me? Raise your hands. Come on. Don't be afraid."

The others slipped around the corner. "No hands?" said Witz. "Nobody with me?"

He waited a moment. And then he followed.

The friends passed fish tank after fish tank. No killer whales anywhere.

Sonny walked up to the front desk. "What's the most awesomest thing here?" he asked a woman.

"Well," she replied. "There's Slappy."

A few moments later, the Stinkers were outside at the sea lion exhibit. They stared at Slappy. He was a sea lion. A chubby, happy sea lion with funny-looking whiskers and bright eyes.

"Sure ain't no killer whale," Loaf said, disappointed.

"Arf!" Slappy gave a joyful bark. He clapped his flippers. He dove for a fish. Then he rolled around and around in the water.

"He's so bummed," Lucy said.

"Huh?" Witz peered at Slappy. "He doesn't look bummed to me."

"You don't understand sea lions," Sonny explained.

A smile spread across Slappy's face.

"He could die in there," said Domino.

"Yeah, right." Witz snorted.

Loaf shook his head. "The ocean is his home. That's where he belongs."

Sonny nodded. "We've got to free him."

"Free him?" Witz couldn't believe it. "We don't even know him."

Domino smiled. *"Free Willy . . . Free Slappy."*

Sonny squared his shoulders. "If one kid can free a whale, then five can free a sea lion."

5

Roy walked around the aquarium. He stopped at the octopus tank. "Here boy . . . or girl," he called. "Come play with Uncle Roy."

Roy waited. No octopus. So he dangled his bus keys over the tank.

A tentacle shot out of the water. It grabbed the keys. Then it disappeared.

"Hey, octopus!" Roy called again. "Give them back."

Nothing.

Sighing, Roy took off his hat. He held it

over the tank. He waited for the octopus to surface.

But those keys were not to be seen.

Mr. Brinway was droning on and on. Students napped on the floor. They leaned against walls. Nobody was listening.

"Mr. Brinway," Spencer interrupted.

Annoyed, Mr. Brinway snapped, "What?" Then he saw it was Spencer.

"What's wrong, son?" he asked gently.

"The Stinkers are gone!" Spencer tattled.

Mr. Brinway stopped talking.

The Stinkers were planning the Slappy breakout. Should they use a giant crane? Swim through sewers?

No, those ideas wouldn't work.

Tag came into Slappy's yard. He prodded Slappy to go inside. The Stinkers couldn't see what was behind the door.

"Hey!" Lucy said. "That man is taking Slappy!"

"Forget Slappy!" Witz exclaimed. "Here comes Mr. Brinway!"

Mr. Brinway charged through the doors. "Stinkers, freeze!" he ordered.

The Stinkers exchanged looks. "I say we freeze," Witz offered. "How many are with me?"

"Run!" Sonny declared.

Everyone raced back into the aquarium.

Mr. Brinway bolted after them. "Where are those Stinkers?" he muttered. He checked the seashell exhibit. Near the lobster tanks. Then he ducked into the gift shop.

They weren't near the books . . . or the postcards . . . or the fish masks. He headed into the poster section.

"Wait," he said loudly. "There's something fishy about those masks."

He stopped to laugh at his joke. In a flash, the Stinkers looked out from under their masks. They dashed for the door.

A second later they flew past Roy and the octopus tank.

"Hi, Roy!" said Sonny as they swept past. They raced around a girl, another man, and then a boy.

"Oops!" said Witz. They knocked the boy's skateboard to the floor. But they didn't have time to stop. Sonny flung open a side door. And everyone rushed inside.

Mr. Brinway breathed hard, trying to keep up. He sped by Roy. Then he slipped on something. The skateboard! He rolled forward. "Oh!" he cried, flipping off . . . over Roy's head . . .

Splash! Into the octopus tank.

Slowly, Mr. Brinway rose out of the water. The octopus was stuck on his face. And the octopus held the keys in one tentacle.

6

In a back room, Sonny crept out of hiding. "I think we lost him," he told the others.

Domino, Lucy, and Loaf came out from behind some boxes. Witz followed a second later. "Arf!" Witz jumped. That sound. It wasn't Mr. Brinway. It was coming from a crate. . . . It was . . .

Sonny flipped off the cover. Slappy!

"Oh, he's in a cage. Poor little baby," cooed Lucy. She bent close to the sea lion. Slappy stuck out his nose. He nuzzled her

This is Slappy, the most lovable — and smelliest — sea lion in the world!

Meet the Stinkers:

Sonny De Silva

Lucy O'Hara

Domino Dupree

Loaf concocts a new invention, and the Stinkers try it out on Witz.

Morgan Brinway is the headmaster at Dartmoor Academy. He has no patience for the Stinkers' antics.

Dartmoor 'Acade

Pride, prestige and prosperity

for your progeny

1938

ville

"You

usines

The Stinkers are going to save Slappy from his life at the aquarium — whether he likes it or not!

Unfortunately, a mean crook, Tony Boccoli, wants to steal Slappy and sell him to a circus.

Since Slappy won't go back in the ocean, the Stinkers hide him in Mr. Brinway's hot tub.

After all that work, Slappy needs a nap.

With Tony Boccoli chasing them, the Stinkers make a getaway car — out of a bathtub!

Finally the tub stops at the edge of an old log flume.

There's no place to go but down.

In the end, Mr. Brinway learns to like the Stinkers — and Slappy!

cheek. "You want to go home?" Lucy asked. "To the ocean?"

"Arf! Arf!" Slappy barked.

"It's fate," Sonny said. "We have to free him!" He opened the cage.

Outside, Boccoli stood on the loading dock. He was arguing with Tag. "Don't say forget it," said Boccoli. He waved at a cage and a pile of fish.

"I'm ready for that sea lion. I've got to have him."

"But I almost got caught," Tag said. "Get him yourself."

Tag opened the door to go inside. "Arf!" Slappy burst into the bright sunshine. The door slammed shut. Click. It locked the Stinkers inside.

Boccoli pushed Slappy into the tiny cage. It was so easy, Tag decided to help. Then he grabbed the money. "You're on your own," he told Boccoli. And he disappeared inside.

Boccoli sighed. He had to get his van.

And there'd be no one to watch Slappy. "Don't go nowhere, fatso," he commanded. Glancing over his shoulder, he left.

Just then the Stinkers rounded the corner. They had managed to break out of the room. They spotted the cage.

"It's Slappy!" Lucy cried. "Isn't this great?"

"Great isn't the word," moaned Witz.

"Don't worry." Sonny reached in to pat Slappy's head. He swept up the pile of fish. "We'll get you out."

A minute later Boccoli drove up. But Slappy was gone.

7

Loaf walked backward in front of Slappy. Every few steps he held out a fish. Slappy waddled forward. He snatched each and every one — until he waddled onto the bus.

"Guys," said Witz. "Isn't someone going to notice this? I mean Slappy is a big, fat, smelly sea lion."

Slappy glared at him.

"Sorry, Slappy," Witz apologized. "You're really a good-looking sea lion."

Slappy smiled.

"He needs a disguise," Sonny decided.

Loaf peeled off his Dartmoor sweat-shirt. Everyone squeezed and heaved and pushed Slappy into it. They snapped a shark mask over his face. Then Loaf crouched under the seat so Slappy could pretend to be him! But the Stinkers still couldn't hide Slappy's smell. The odor floated through the bus.

"Boy," Spencer shouted when everyone had gotten on. "One of you Stinkers really stinks!"

Roy opened the window. Mr. Brinway huddled in his seat, cold and wet. He shot the Stinkers a dirty look. They were sitting there nice and quiet. Looking so sweet in their masks. But his octopus swim was all their fault!

Screech! Boccoli tore into the parking lot. As the bus pulled past, he read the name "Dartmoor Academy."

Hmmm, he thought. Dartmoor.

Back at Dartmoor, the Stinkers had another problem. What would they do with Slappy now?

"Mr. Brinway's hot tub!" exclaimed Sonny.

They headed across campus to Mr. Brinway's house. Slappy waddled behind. Roy had used fish fertilizer on the grass and Slappy was digging it up to eat it. He was leaving a long deep rut.

Witz shuffled along. Using Mr. Brinway's backyard? That was just crazy! First they had to climb a fence to get in. And what if somebody was there?

"Yip! Yip!" Witz jumped. Somebody was at the house! But it was only Brinway's little dog, Gordon.

The dog scampered through a doggy door. He disappeared inside the house. Witz let out a breath. Now it was safe.

The Stinkers gathered around the hot tub. "Look, Slappy." Lucy coaxed him closer. "It's water. Just like home."

Slappy turned up his nose.

"Maybe it's too hot," said Sonny. "And Slappy probably likes saltwater."

The Stinkers crawled into the kitchen

through the doggy door. Sonny found a big bag of salt. Domino took ice cubes from the freezer. The Stinkers poured everything into the tub.

Domino tested the water. "Perfect! Come on, Slap."

Slappy shook his head.

"If you go in," said Loaf. "We'll give you more fish."

Slappy dove right in.

Witz checked the fish supply. "We've got trouble," he told the others. "There is no F-I-S-H," he spelled out.

Slappy leaped out of the water. Slap, slap, slap went his flippers. Furious, he splashed the Stinkers.

"This is scary!" Lucy whispered. "He can spell!"

There was only one thing to do. Order a load of fish from Barney the Buccaneer. And while they were at it, they ordered some fries.

The food came a little while later. The Stinkers fed Slappy. They played catch and tag. They laughed and joked and munched on fries.

Finally Witz checked his watch. It was almost five.

"Guys," he said. "I hate to mess up a good time — "

"Come on, Witz. You love it," Loaf joked.

"But we have to get back to school," Witz went on. "My mom will have a cow if I'm not there."

"Stay there, Slappy," Sonny told the sea lion. "We'll be back soon."

Slappy nodded and dove for another fish.

"What about Mr. Brinway?" asked Witz.

Sonny laughed. "He never leaves early."

8

At that same moment, Mr. Brinway stood up. "I'm going home early," he told Harriet. He shivered. He was still wet from his dunk in the octopus tank. And the next day was Parents' Day at school. He needed to rest.

Mr. Brinway hugged his jacket closer. Then he trudged to his car.

"Mr. Brinway!" Roy called. He checked the long trench in the ground once again. It had to be a gopher hole, he decided. What else could it be?

He pulled up to Mr. Brinway on his lawn mower. "I don't want to start a panic," he said. "But there's a humongous gopher here. Five or six feet long!"

Mr. Brinway shielded his car. Roy and his lawn mower made him nervous. "A six-foot gopher?" he repeated. "Oh, yes. And have you seen that fifty-foot chipmunk?" He snickered. Then he drove quickly away.

Roy scratched his head. "Fifty-foot chipmunk? He's really nuts."

Mr. Brinway turned the heat on in the car. He kept his eyes straight ahead. He didn't notice the black van. Or the big man sitting inside.

At the house, Gordon raced up to Mr. Brinway.

"Yip! Yip!" The dog jumped up and down.

"Not now, Gordon," Mr. Brinway said. "Daddy doesn't want to play."

Slappy had his head in the refrigerator. Slurp! Slurp! He snuffled up everything in sight. Head down, Mr. Brinway shuffled past.

Mr. Brinway paused in the hallway. Should he go back to the kitchen? Get something to eat?

No, he decided. He'd change out of his wet clothes. He'd put on some music.

A few minutes later, opera music filled the house. Mr. Brinway came out of the bedroom. He wore a bathing suit and a robe and a matching blue bathing cap. He smiled, thinking about the hot tub. How good it would feel to relax.

"Arf!" Slappy barked. "Arf!" He waddled out of the kitchen — just as Mr. Brinway walked in.

"That's some bark," Mr. Brinway told Gordon. "Are you getting a cold?"

"Whoops!" He slipped on an ice cube and flew into the air. Thud! Mr. Brinway landed flat on his back. "Better get that ice maker fixed," he muttered. He stood up and rubbed his back. "Oh, I need that hot tub. Right now."

Mr. Brinway hurried into the tub. "Owww!" He shot up fast. "Brr! That's cold." He lowered himself in again slowly.

"This water tastes salty. And fishy!"

Just then Sonny peeked over the fence. "Brinway is in the hot tub," he told his friends.

Witz gasped. "With Slappy?"

"No, with himself."

"Then where's Slappy?" Lucy asked.

The Stinkers peered through every window. Finally they spotted Slappy in the living room. *Zzzzz*. He was fast asleep on the recliner.

The Stinkers nodded. They saw him. Now they just had to get him.

Mr. Brinway climbed out of the tub. Then he noticed a crumpled paper wrapper. It said "Barney the Buccaneer."

"That's it!" he cried. "People had a party here. They changed the temperature in the hot tub. They ate fish!" He stormed into the kitchen to call the police.

Sonny jumped down into the yard. He stole inside behind Mr. Brinway.

B-r-i-n-g! The doorbell rang. Mr. Brinway tugged his robe closed. He flung open the door.

No one was there.

"That's strange," Mr. Brinway said. He stepped outside to investigate.

Bang! The door slammed shut. Mr. Brinway twisted around. His robe was stuck! He pulled the door. It was locked!

"Gordon!" he shouted. He pounded the door. "Let me in!" Then he realized. Gordon was a dog.

Mr. Brinway slipped out of his robe. He peered left. He peered right. Then he dashed around the house . . . into the backyard.

The front door swung open. Sonny popped out, tugging Slappy behind him. The other Stinkers leaped into the open. They hurried to help.

"What will we do with him now?" asked Loaf.

Everyone turned to Witz.

9

"Why me?" Witz asked. He was home in bed. The blanket was pulled up to his chin. Slappy lay next to him. His nose poked out of the covers.

"Why does Slappy have to stay with me?"

The other Stinkers stood outside the window. "Because you're the one with a double bed," explained Sonny.

The Stinkers waved good-bye. "And don't make a sound," Sonny warned. "Not even a wheeze. It will get Slappy excited."

Witz froze. He didn't move a muscle. Who knew what Slappy would do?

Then he felt it. A wheeze coming on. He clamped his mouth shut. He tried to hold it in.

HONK!

Slappy jerked his head. He barked. Once. Twice. Loud and louder. Witz groaned. He heard his mom in the hallway.

Quickly he tossed a blanket over Slappy.

Mrs. Witzowitz opened the door. "I don't like that cough," she told Witz.

Witz coughed. "Arf! Arf!"

Did he sound enough like a sea lion?

Mrs. Witzowitz wrinkled her nose. "What did you eat today? Fish? It must have upset your stomach." Then she glanced at the blanket. "And what's that lump?"

She pulled back the cover. Witz waited for the shriek.

Nothing.

Slappy had disappeared.

Mrs. Witzowitz shook her head. "Any-

40

way, I'm going to give you Z-Lax Junior. It will help your stomach."

Witz hid a shudder. That medicine! It meant going to the bathroom. A lot.

"Yes, Mom," he said obediently.

Mrs. Witzowitz handed him a square from a Z-Lax bar. "Good night, honey," she said. She closed the door behind her.

Witz jumped out of bed. He looked under the bed. Slappy swung his head out, and gave him a big wet kiss.

"Yuck!" Witz rubbed his face. "Sea lion slobber."

G-r-r-r. Witz's stomach rumbled. "I have to go to the bathroom," he told Slappy. "I hope you're happy." He pushed him back under the bed. "Stay here. And keep quiet."

As soon as Witz left, Slappy popped out. He spotted the Z-Lax bar. Mmm-mm. Slappy smiled. He sucked it down one, two, three.

G-R-R-R went his stomach. G-R-R-R!

Slappy raced into the bathroom, too.

10

That night Roy dressed in black. He put on special night goggles. Then he opened a box marked, "Gopher Bombs."

He was ready.

Roy crept out of his shed. He had the bombs in one hand. The launcher in the other. Where was that giant gopher?

On the other side of the fence, Boccoli squinted in the dark. He tossed over a big fish. Then he started to climb.

"I've got to start exercising." He panted

and struggled to the top. Suddenly he lost his balance. His arms flailed. He fell over.

Thud! His glasses flew off his nose.

Meanwhile, Roy crawled along the ground. He stopped. Did he hear something by the fence? A gopher?

"Where are my glasses?" Boccoli muttered. He felt along the ground. He couldn't see a thing.

His hand touched something. Was that it? He grabbed it. He tried to put it on his nose.

"Pew!" he said. It was the fish.

Roy peered through his goggles. He spied something big, creeping on the ground. The gopher!

Roy snuck closer. He gripped the launcher. He took aim and let the bomb fly.

Boccoli reached for something else on the ground. His glasses! Smiling, he put them on. He could see! He could see . . . a smoking bomb coming right at him!

Boom!

Roy rushed up a second later. "Missed him." He sighed. There was nothing there.

Boccoli had flung himself over the fence. His clothes were burned to black.

And the fish was fried.

11

Witz woke up early in the morning. He sprayed the bathroom with air freshener. Again. Nothing like a sick sea lion, he thought. Then he snuck Slappy out of the house.

The Stinkers gathered in the woods near Dartmoor. The plan: To bring Slappy home. To take him to the ocean.

Loaf rubbed his hands together. He had the perfect invention to do it. A bathtub on wheels. Loaf hooked a rope from the tub to his bicycle. And it was set.

"One, two, three," said Sonny, giving the tub a push. Away they rolled. The Stinkers grinned. It worked! Smiling, they climbed on their bikes.

The bathtub swayed and bounced along the road. Slappy moaned, sick to his stomach.

The friends biked along the coast. Below them, the ocean sparkled. Waves lapped a sandy beach.

Sonny led the Stinkers to the shore. "Look, Slappy," he said, pointing to the ocean.

The water stretched so far, you couldn't see the end.

Slappy hid his head.

"This is it," Sonny told him. "You're home."

Slappy covered his eyes. This wasn't the aquarium. He tried to grip the tub with his flippers. To stay inside. But the Stinkers hauled him out.

They pushed Slappy across the sand. They reached the water, and stopped.

Foamy waves sloshed their sneakers.

For a moment, they gazed at the sea lion. "I'm going to miss you Slappy," said Lucy. She gave him a hug.

Domino patted his head. "Me too, Slap."

"So am I," Loaf added.

Sonny's voice shook. "We're all going to miss you."

"I'm not," Witz said loudly. "No offense," he told Slappy. "But seeing you on my toilet? That was quite enough!"

Sonny held out a fish. He wanted to give Slappy one last meal.

Slappy shook his head. He didn't want it!

"Something's wrong," said Domino.

"No," Lucy said. "There's bazillions of fish in the ocean. Slappy knows it. Dive in," she urged.

"Arf!" Slappy backed away.

The Stinkers pushed. They prodded. And they pulled. Slappy didn't budge.

Suddenly they heard a splash. A killer whale leaped out of the water. It hung for a moment in the air. Then it dove back down.

Everyone stared, openmouthed. Slappy's eyes grew wide with fear.

"It's Willy!" said Sonny. "Don't you want to be with Willy?"

Slappy trembled.

"Wait!" Loaf said. "Don't killer whales eat sea lions?"

"Arf!" Slappy nodded.

The whale surfaced again. Closer this time. Water shot out of its blowhole.

Slappy jumped into the tub.

The Stinkers sighed. No way could they send Slappy into the ocean. They needed another plan.

"I say we free Slappy," Witz told the others. "Back into the aquarium."

Slappy clapped his flippers.

"You're right," said Sonny.

"I am?" Witz was surprised.

Sonny smiled. "We'll unmess our mess. We'll take Slappy back to the aquarium. His real home."

12

Back at Dartmoor, Mr. Brinway marched across campus. He wore a sea captain's uniform. It was for the opera they'd be putting on later. A ship bobbed on an outdoor stage, ready for the performance.

It was Parents' Day.

Mr. Brinway held up his megaphone. "Show time everyone!" he announced. The parents would be there any minute. And Mr. Brinway wanted everything to be perfect.

Mr. Brinway nodded. The food booths

looked great. The spin art booth did too. Frisbees whirled, spraying paint onto paper.

He checked the Ping-Pong toss. Again, Mr. Brinway nodded. Bowls of goldfish for prizes. Now, that was a nice touch.

Finally he passed the Moon Bounce. He instructed Roy to make sure it was well filled with air.

Everything is going smoothly, Mr. Brinway thought.

The Stinkers weren't even around. If he were lucky, they wouldn't show at all.

Parents began to arrive. Mr. Brinway smiled. Now where was Spencer Dane, Sr.? This was his chance. He would get Spencer's dad to join the board. Then he'd be sure to donate money for the Brinway Music Festival.

"Ah," Mr. Brinway said to himself. "There he is. Talking to Harriet."

Mr. Brinway strolled over. "Call me Spence," Spencer's dad was saying. He smiled at Harriet.

"I've been meaning to ask you, Mr. Dane," Mr. Brinway began. He trailed off. He waited for the man to say, "Call me Spence."

Spencer's father just looked at him. Finally he snapped. "What is it, Brinway?" When Mr. Brinway didn't answer right away, he stalked off.

"We'll talk later," Mr. Brinway called after him.

A large man in black glasses swept past Mr. Brinway.

Boccoli.

"Great school," he muttered, trying to fit in.

Mr. Brinway ignored him. His eyes narrowed. What was that he heard? Familiar voices. Voices he knew all too well.

The Stinkers.

The five friends hurried through the crowd. "Maybe we should have stayed with Slappy," said Lucy. "He seemed hungry."

"He'll be fine," Sonny told her. "Right where he is."

Meanwhile, Roy edged around the parents. Just outside his shed, he stopped in his tracks.

"Arf!"

The gopher! It was hiding in the tall grass. Roy dropped to his stomach. He slithered through the blades.

"Arf!"

Roy followed the barks. They were getting louder. And closer. Roy sprang forward and when he looked into the tall grass . . .

Slappy looked down.

"Ahhh!" Roy screamed.

"Ahhh!" Slappy screamed back. He had leaped out of the tub, and now . . . waddle, waddle, waddle. He scuttled away.

"That gopher's bigger than I thought!" said Roy. He hitched up his pants. He grabbed his hedge trimmer. And he took off after him.

13

Slappy scurried through the grass. He sniffed. Then he smiled. Fish! There were fish nearby!

Slappy waddled to the booths. He poked his head into the back of the Ping-Pong toss. Twenty-five goldfish swam in twenty-five bowls. A feast!

Slappy lunged for the table.

"Oh!" a woman screamed. Children dropped their Ping Pong balls and ran.

Slappy stuffed his snout into a bowl.

"Oww!" he cried. He was stuck. He couldn't reach the fish!

Whimpering, he pushed off the bowl. He sat in the middle of the goldfish. Stumped. How could he get them?

Suddenly Roy leaped into the booth. Vroom! He revved his hedge trimmer. The blade shook with power.

Slappy bolted. "Arf!" Slappy raced past Sonny and his mom.

"Wasn't that a sea lion?" she asked.

"I didn't see nothing," Sonny said quickly.

Slappy skittered past Boccoli. Boccoli squinted. The sea lion!

Slappy whizzed past Domino and his dad.

Slappy and Roy skidded into the pastry booth. Roy vaulted onto the table. Stamp! Stamp! He stomped all over tubes of icing. Squirt! Red, green, and yellow cream squeezed out.

They sped past Spencer, who was all alone on the Moon Bounce.

Standing in the crowd, Mr. Brinway

peered around. What was all the commotion? Was Roy chasing a sea lion?

"I got the gopher, Mr. Brinway!" shouted Roy. "He's in the bushes!"

Mr. Brinway grabbed the hedge trimmer. "That's not a gopher," he hissed. He swung the trimmer away from Roy.

R-r-r-i-p! The trimmer tore into the Moon Bounce.

Pfffft! The Moon Bounce began to deflate like a giant balloon. It sputtered and slid across the ground. The terrified astronaut held on tight.

"No!" screamed Mr. Brinway. "This isn't happening!"

The runaway Moon Bounce careened through the crowds. It crashed through the Parents' Day banner. Thump! It smashed into the spin art booth. Paint cans flew into the air. Spencer Jr. flew out and he and his father dove for cover. But it was too late. The paint rained down, covering them in red, blue, yellow, and green from head to toe.

"Arf!" Slappy barked weakly. He was slowing down.

The Stinkers hurried over. "Don't hurt Slappy!" Lucy cried.

"Stay out of this," Mr. Brinway warned. "He's a dangerous beast."

"No, he's not," said Loaf. "He's our friend."

"Brinway," Spencer, Sr. shouted. He strode over and glared. Paint dripped off him, falling to the ground.

"It-it-it's not my fault," Mr. Brinway stammered. "It was the Stinkers. And their friend, Sloppy."

"I think it's Slappy," Roy corrected.

But Spencer didn't want to hear any excuses. He stormed off. Mr. Brinway watched helplessly.

"There goes the Brinway Music Festival," he said.

14

Slappy gazed at the crowds. At Mr. Brinway. "Arf!" he barked. He broke free. The Stinkers raced after him into the woods.

"Slappy, wait!" Lucy called. "Nobody's going to hurt you."

Boccoli jumped out from behind a tree. He caught hold of Slappy. Before the Stinkers could stop him, Boccoli snapped a leash around Slappy's neck. "Got'cha!" he cried.

"Who are you?" Sonny demanded, catching up.

"I'm from the aquarium," Boccoli lied. "And I'm taking this sea lion back."

Boccoli jerked the leash. Slappy grunted. He pulled back. Lucy could tell he didn't like this man.

"The leash is too tight," she told him. "You're choking him."

"Better get back," Boccoli threatened. "He'll bite."

Sonny gave him a funny look. "He wouldn't bite anybody."

"Yeah," Witz said. He stepped forward. "Leave him alone."

Boccoli glared at Witz. "You're lucky I don't have you arrested. On seal-napping charges."

"Seal-napping charges? Jail? No good." Witz stepped back.

Sonny petted Slappy softly. "You're going home," he said.

The sea lion whimpered. He looked pleadingly at the Stinkers.

"Don't worry," Lucy shouted after him. "We'll visit!"

The Stinkers heard one last little cry. And Slappy was gone.

No more little barks. No more smiles. No more Slappy. The Stinkers trudged back to campus.

Witz sighed. He was going to miss that crazy sea lion. No matter how much trouble he'd been.

And speaking of trouble . . . he thought.

Dartmoor campus was in shambles. Booths were torn apart. Food and paint and paper littered the grounds.

Mr. Brinway paced in front of the deflated Moon Bounce. All the Stinkers' parents gathered around him.

"My beautiful school," he groaned. "It looks like a war zone." He pointed at the friends as they came closer. "And you Stinkers did it."

Sonny stepped forward. He looked Mr. Brinway in the eye. "We wanted to help Slappy," he told him. "It was my idea, sir. So if you want to blame someone, blame me."

"And me," said Lucy.

"And me," said Domino.

"And me," said Loaf.

Witz gazed at his feet. "I guess me, too."

Mr. Brinway sneered. "Very touching. But you're all expelled. For life!"

15

Expelled! For once, the Stinkers were quiet. Slowly they walked to their cars.

A van pulled up beside them. It said Springfield Aquarium on the side. The Stinkers exchanged looks. Was it that man again? Had he come back?

A different man jumped out, and a woman.

"We got a call about a sea lion," the woman, Nancy, said.

"You're too late," Domino told her. "Some

guy from the aquarium already picked him up."

The man, Tommy, frowned. "That's impossible. What did he look like?"

Loaf said, "Big. Ugly. Thick glasses. Greasy hair."

"Sounds like Anthony Boccoli got his sea lion," Nancy said with a sigh. "He bribed a worker to get Slappy. Now he's going to sell Slappy to a circus. One that doesn't take care of animals."

Sonny's face turned pale. "You're going to save him. Right?"

Tommy shook his head. "I wish we could. But the police don't have time. And we don't have money or people to track him down. We can only hope he's okay."

The Stinkers exchanged looks. Lucy hugged herself tight. This was so awful! So horrible.

And there was nothing they could do.

16

The next day the Stinkers biked to Dartmoor. They were still expelled. But they wanted to be together. So they met in Roy's shed.

"Hey, Roy," said Sonny. "Is it okay we're here?"

"Sure," Roy answered. "Just don't let Brinway see you." He gazed at the Stinkers one by one. "You all seem down."

"It's Slappy," Lucy said.

Sonny nodded. "First we freed him. And he didn't need to be freed. Then we gave him to a bad man. Now he needs to be freed. And we can't do a thing."

Witz kicked a pebble. "We're losers," he said. "Just like Max and Spencer thought."

Slowly Roy stood up. He turned serious. "That's enough," he told them. "You guys are Stinkers. That means something. Every kid wants to be a Stinker. But they don't have the guts."

The Stinkers stared back.

"You're special," Roy continued. "So raise your heads up high."

He paused to look at the friends. "There now. How do you feel?"

"Lousy," said Lucy.

Roy shrugged. "Sometimes it works. Sometimes it doesn't."

Witz slumped against the lawn mower. "Slappy must be a million miles away," he said.

"Maybe not," Roy put in.

The Stinkers perked up.

"Do you think Boccoli lives around here?" Sonny asked.

"Why not?" Roy answered. "You do."

"Yeah, we do." Domino grinned. Maybe there was something to this.

Loaf picked up the gopher bomb launcher. He eyed a stack of potatoes.

You never know, he thought. If we find Boccoli? This could come in handy.

17

The Stinkers had work to do. They had to find Boccoli. But where would they look?

"One thing is for sure," Loaf told the others. "He needs a lot of fish."

The Stinkers nodded. They jumped on their bikes. Ten minutes later they stood at the docks. Fish stand after fish stand lined the crowded alley.

The Stinkers gazed around. It was so hard to see. They'd have to check everywhere. Scout the area.

The Stinkers raced from stand to stand. From dockhand to dockhand.

No one had seen Boccoli. No one could help.

Disappointed, the Stinkers sat on a curb. What would they do now? Lucy lifted her head to think — and saw Boccoli.

He was standing at the other end of the alley. Dockhands loaded fish into his van. Boccoli handed money to a large woman. Then he drove away.

The Stinkers ran over. "Excuse me," Sonny said to the woman. "But we know that man. Did he say where he lives?"

"That creep!" the woman said. "He's living in the old sawmill on Mud Mountain."

The Stinkers rushed to their bikes. But Witz hung back. "We can't go to Mud Mountain," he called to the others. "Boccoli will kill us."

Sonny stopped. He turned to Witz. "We got Slappy into this. We have to get him out."

"We're all Slappy has," Domino said.

"Yeah," Lucy added. "We're his family. And families stick together."

"Remember what Roy said?" asked Loaf. "We're Stinkers. And that means something."

Witz thought about Boccoli. About the danger. Then he pictured Slappy. Smiling. Eating. Barking.

"Let's rumble!" he cried.

18

The sawmill looked deserted. The Stinkers stood outside. They gazed around the logging camp. Rusty pieces of machinery lay scattered on the ground. Big logs were strewn everywhere.

The Stinkers separated. They each worked quickly. Quietly.

Then they met behind a giant log.

"It's a go!" Sonny whispered. He lifted Mr. Brinway's megaphone.

Inside the mill, Boccoli eyed the unhappy sea lion. Slappy perched on a barrel. He wore a clown hat and a bright red nose. A flaming hoop stood before him.

Slappy shook with fear.

Boccoli poked him with a long stick. "You want to eat?" he jeered. "Then jump through the hoop! I promised the circus a trained seal!"

Boccoli jabbed Slappy again. Slappy leaped. He sailed into the air. But he missed the hoop. Splat! He landed flat on his belly.

"You stink!" Boccoli shouted. "Get up! Get up!" He lifted the stick.

A loud voice stopped him. "Anthony Boccoli. You are surrounded by police and Marines. Come out with your hands up."

Boccoli chained Slappy to a beam. It ran from the floor to the ceiling. "There," Boccoli muttered. "That should hold you." Then he lumbered outside.

Sonny stood in the middle of the camp. Holding a megaphone. Alone.

"You're in trouble, kid." Boccoli sneered.

He waved his stick and lurched forward.

"Now!" Sonny shouted.

Lucy jumped out of hiding. She aimed a giant hose. Water gushed out, drenching Boccoli.

"What?" he cried.

Witz turned on the leaf blower. Domino emptied a box of sawdust right in front of it. Whoosh! A cloud of dust zoomed through the air. It covered Boccoli from head to toe. He tried to pick at the wood shavings. They were stuck fast.

Boccoli dropped his stick. He wiped his glasses clean. Pffft! Sonny launched a potato right at him. A direct hit! Pffft! Another potato smashed into his stomach. Boccoli doubled over.

"I'm being attacked by the seven dwarfs," he gasped.

He glared at Sonny, Domino, Lucy, and Witz. They all stood together in a line, glaring back.

"I'll kill you," Boccoli screamed. He charged straight for them.

"Wait," Sonny whispered. "Wait . . . wait . . . now!"

At the last second, the four friends scattered.

"Surprise!" cried Loaf. He gripped a giant saw at one end. A big rock held down the other end. Loaf let go. Boing! The saw sprang forward. It hit Boccoli smack on the nose.

The big man crumpled to the ground. Quickly, Lucy and Witz looped a rope around his ankles. Domino tied the other end around a barrel filled with rocks at the edge of a deep well. The barrel teetered on the edge of the well. Domino was pushing the barrel. He pushed and pushed, expecting the barrel to fall down. To take Boccoli with it.

Nothing happened.

All at once, Boccoli jumped to his feet. He grabbed Lucy's foot.

Lucy tried to scoot back. But Boccoli held her fast. "Let me go!" she shouted.

Boccoli pulled her closer. And closer.

"Witz!" Lucy pleaded. "Help me!"

Witz gritted his teeth. He flung himself at Boccoli. He wrapped his legs around his neck.

"Argh!" Boccoli choked. He tumbled backward. In a flash, Lucy scrambled free. But Boccoli locked his arms around Witz.

Meanwhile, Domino was still pushing. "I'm too skinny!" he shouted at Sonny and Loaf. They pushed, too. The barrel edged forward.

Boccoli gripped Witz hard. He jerked at the rope at his feet. He was loosening it. Freeing himself.

Witz closed his eyes. "I'm finished," he moaned. "I'm dead."

The rope suddenly tightened. It dug into Boccoli's ankles.

"Hey!" he shouted, as he was yanked backward into the air.

Witz opened his eyes. "I'm alive!" he exclaimed. Boccoli swung upside down in the sawmill doorway.

"Witz!" Lucy hugged him. "You saved me. You're a hero."

Witz shrugged. "It was nothing. Well. Okay. It was something."

"Get me down!" Boccoli yelled.

The Stinkers rushed around him. They skidded to a stop inside the mill.

"Slappy!" they cried. He looked so . . . so silly.

"Arf!" he barked happily.

Slappy nuzzled Lucy. He gave Witz a kiss.

"All right, all right." Witz laughed. "You're welcome."

Sonny tugged on Slappy's chain. "We have to bust this."

Domino spied a large hammer in the corner. He and Loaf lugged it over. Bang! They slammed it down. Sparks flew. But the chain held fast.

"Oh!" Lucy screamed. She pointed at the doorway. "He's back!"

Boccoli loomed before them. His clothes

were in shreds. His hair stood on end. And his nose was the size of a beach ball.

"It's over," he declared. He grabbed Sonny by the shirt. "Arf!" Slappy rammed into Boccoli, full force. Boccoli staggered. He grazed the hoop with the seat of his pants.

"Ow!" he cried, jumping up and down. "Hot! Hot!"

In a rush, the Stinkers led Slappy outside.

"Arf!" Slappy jerked to a stop. He was still chained!

"Pull, Slappy," everyone cried. "Pull!" Slappy took a deep breath. He dove forward with all his might. Again and again.

Boccoli staggered to his feet. He stumbled to the door.

"Arf!" Slappy yanked the chain. The chain pulled the beam. Creak! The beam bent. Further and further. Thwack! Slappy tore it right out of the floor.

Crash! Bang! Boom! The roof fell in. The

sawmill collapsed like a house of cards.

The Stinkers stared in shock. It was nothing but a heap of wood.

"Arf!" Slappy was still stuck. The chain was buried under the pile.

"Wait a minute," Loaf said. He slipped the collar over Slappy's head. It was that easy.

Creak! Something moved . . . the pile of rubble shifted. Boccoli crawled out.

"That guy is like the Terminator," Domino said, amazed. "But blind."

The Stinkers didn't have a moment to lose. They raced to the woods. Quickly, they pulled branches off the old bathtub. It was their only hope.

"Are you sure this will work?" Witz asked Loaf.

"I've added hockey stick brakes and a steering wheel," said Loaf. "Sure I'm sure. I think."

Everyone climbed inside. Loaf sat in a seat in the back to work the brakes. Sonny scooted behind the wheel.

And they were off!

19

The Stinkers rolled down the steep mountain road. Faster and faster. They were gaining speed. The road twisted and turned. Witz closed his eyes, afraid to peek.

Vroom! Boccoli and his van sped up behind them. Boccoli gunned the engine. He slammed into the tub. One brake splintered.

Loaf dove out of the backseat. "Thought I'd sit here for a while," he said to Witz, nose to nose.

Sonny peered over his shoulder. Boccoli was about to ram them again. Quickly he jerked the wheel. The tub swerved off the road. Bump! It hit an old logging trail. And kept picking up speed.

Snap! Branches whipped in their faces. Wind lashed their faces. But maybe they had lost Boccoli.

Witz glanced back and groaned. He was hot on their tracks.

A little way down the trail, all was peaceful. Mr. Brinway sighed happily. He was leading a bird-watching field trip. Without the Stinkers! Nothing could go wrong.

Harriet and Roy turned their heads. They'd heard a strange rumbling. It wasn't Gordon. He sat at their feet, wagging his tail. "Mr. Brinway," said Roy. "Did you hear that?"

"Quiet!" Mr. Brinway hissed. "It could be a common loon. Very rare. Don't scare it."

He trained his binoculars up to the sky. Where was that bird?

Screech! The tub burst out of the bushes. "Look out, Mr. Brinway!" shouted Sonny.

Gordon jumped into Mr. Brinway's arms, just as the tub barreled into him.

"Ayiii!" Mr. Brinway cried, flipping high into the air and landing on the backseat. A few seconds later Gordon came down and landed right in Roy's arms! Gordon barked happily. He licked Roy's face.

"Stop this tub!" ordered Mr. Brinway. But the Stinkers couldn't listen. Boccoli was closing in.

The tub bounced and jounced down the trail. Suddenly Sonny sucked in his breath. Up ahead! They were heading for a shed!

20

The tub sailed into the shed. Bang! It bumped up a ramp.

Witz choked back a cry. He knew what this led to. A flume. A giant slide used to send logs down the mountain.

Down the mountain? And they only had one brake!

Loaf leaned hard on the hockey stick. R-r-r-r. It dug into the bottom of the ramp.

Not deep enough, thought Witz.

The tub kept going. It slowed down a little. Then a little more. It skidded to the end of the ramp. Finally it stopped, but it was hanging over the edge.

The Stinkers peered down. The flume dropped sharply down the mountainside . . . it was a long scary ride into a deep, deep lake.

The tub teetered forward. They were going over!

Everyone leaned back. The tub teetered back.

Vroom! An engine roared behind them. They heard a door slam. Footsteps.

Lucy peered around. Boccoli was rushing over. There was only one way to escape.

"We're going down the flume!" Sonny said.

"I'm not," said Mr. Brinway. He rose to his feet.

"Oh, yes, you are," Loaf said. The tub teetered. It tottered. And then it took off like a shot down the flume.

"Heeeelp!" Mr. Brinway wailed.

The drop was so sheer! Witz clutched his stomach.

Boccoli laughed. Then he spotted a water valve. "Turn that," he mumbled, "and water will rush down the flume. They'll really be finished."

Still chuckling, he twisted the wheel. Drip, drip. A trickle of water spurted out. Something clogged the pipe.

Boccoli climbed into the flume. He reached inside the water pipe. Leaves. Twigs, he thought. A beaver's dam was lodged inside. Boccoli tore everything out.

Suddenly, a beaver popped out. He took one look at Boccoli, and bit his already swollen nose!

"Ouch, ouch, ouch!" cried Boccoli. A low rumble filled the air. The pipe creaked and shook. The beaver grinned.

Uh-oh, thought Boccoli. He started to climb out. But it was too late. A tidal wave of water blasted out of the pipe. It carried Boccoli down, down, down . . .

Water rushed around the tub. "This is like an Indiana Jones movie!" Domino shouted.

The flume ended just ahead. Mr. Brinway screamed and hid his face.

Whoosh! The tub launched off the edge. It flew into the air.

"Hit it, Loaf!" yelled Sonny.

Loaf yanked on a cord hanging from a backpack on the shower rod. A pair of shower curtains ballooned out just like a parachute.

The tub jerked once. Then it floated slowly down to the lake.

"Loaf!" Witz exclaimed. "You're a genius."

Mr. Brinway lifted his head. "I'm saved! I'm saved!"

Splash! The tub hit the water.

The Stinkers heard the rush of more water. They turned to the flume. A giant gush was whooshing down — taking Boccoli with it.

Boccoli slipped and slid to the end. Then up, up, up he soared. He flipped in mid-air. And down, down, down, he plummeted. Thud! He smashed on top of a log in the middle of the lake.

Suddenly a rope dropped around him. It lassoed him tight.

Witz's eyes traveled to the other end. Roy! Roy had roped Boccoli! Harriet and all the students stood behind him.

"Yea, Roy!" everyone shouted.

"Arf!" barked Slappy.

21

The news spread fast. Five kids saved Slappy the sea lion! Reporters rushed to the aquarium for a special award presentation.

The Stinkers grinned down from the stage. Mr. Brinway, Harriet, and Roy sat with them.

Mr. Brinway stretched his mouth into a smile. He certainly didn't feel like smiling. The Stinkers were back in school. Still . . . reporters were reporters. They'd write him up in newspapers. Maybe he could get donations for his music festival.

Slappy slapped the water. He dove into a pool near the stage. People clapped and snapped pictures.

Tommy, the aquarium worker, stepped up to the microphone. "Slappy is home," he announced, "and a bad man is in jail. Why? Because of these brave children. I present the Dartmoor Academy with a Presidential Commendation. Mr. Brinway, would you like to accept the award?"

Mr. Brinway leaped to his feet. This would make up for Spencer, Sr. For the Stinkers. For everything. He smiled for the camera.

"Mr. Brinway, let's have a picture of you with Slappy," one of the reporters urged.

Then he moved to the pool. Slappy rose up on his back flippers. Slurp! He kissed Mr. Brinway.

"Yuck!" Mr. Brinway pulled back. But he

slipped in a puddle. "Ahhh!" he cried, doing a back flip into the pool.

He spluttered to the surface. Click, click, snapped the cameras.

The Stinkers laughed. It was the perfect end to the perfect adventure.